Eliza jumped up. "Come on! An animal's in trouble!"

Darwin grabbed her arm. "Wait, Eliza! What about helping your father?"

Eliza looked at the boxes and bit her lip. What could she do? Finally, she turned and walked toward the brush. "I have to help if an animal's in trouble!" she declared. "I'm sure I can do it and still have time to help Dad!"

"I hope you're right," Darwin muttered, hurrying after her.

KLASKY CSUPO, INC.

Based on the TV series *The Wild Thornberrys*® created by Klasky Csupo, Inc.
as seen on *Nickelodeon*®

ISBN 0-439-24182-0

12 11 10 9 8 7 6 5 4 3 2 1   0 1 2 3 4 5/0

Printed in the U.S.A.

First Scholastic printing, November 2000

Two Promises Too Many!

by Adam Beechen
illustrated by Bob Ostrom

SCHOLASTIC INC.

New York Toronto London Auckland Sydney
Mexico City New Delhi Hong Kong

Chapter 1

"Lord Nelson's Trousers!"

At the sound of her father's loud cry, twelve-year-old Eliza Thornberry, her best friend Darwin the chimpanzee, and Donnie the little wild boy raced across her family's campsite where they found Nigel frantically tossing trinkets and tribal objects out of a large cardboard box. "Dad, what's the matter?" Eliza asked.

"I've lost my Lord Willy-Nilly pen!" Nigel

moaned, his red moustache twitching.

Darwin ducked with a screech as a *Pocopa* totem whizzed by his head. "*Zabbada zoom!*" Donnie yelled for good measure.

Nigel had used his Lord Willy-Nilly pen since he was younger than Eliza. On its cap was the head of Lord Willy-Nilly, Nigel's childhood cartoon hero, and for every episode of *Nigel Thornberry's Animal World,* Nigel used the pen to write the beginnings and endings of his scripts. It was like a good luck charm; he just couldn't write with any other pen.

"That's terrible, Dad!" Eliza sympathized. "Is your film on the Knysna lourie done?" The Thornberrys had been camped near the town of Hogsback on South Africa's East Cape for a week filming the colorful bird. The forest was really pretty, with its dense clumps of tall trees that cleared enough at spots to reveal many lakes, ponds, and muddy marshes surrounded by bushes and scrub. There were also many spectacular waterfalls, with names like "Madonna and Child" and "Kettlespout."

And the native Knysna lourie birds were really spectacular! Eliza hadn't even seen them at first, because their green feathers hid them so well in the many trees. But in flight, she could clearly see their beautiful red underwings and white crests. And she could definitely hear their funny "*kow-kow-kow*" call!

"I have to write my closing lines," Nigel answered. "Your mother's in the Commvee editing the footage, and the courier plane is coming to collect the film! I can't imagine where the pen went. Just yesterday I was showing it to Donnie!" Nigel bent close to Donnie.

"You haven't seen it, have you, lad?"

Donnie scratched his head, seemingly as puzzled as Nigel. "Don't worry, Dad," Eliza assured him. "We'll help you find it! I promise!"

Nigel held her by the shoulders. "Oh, will you? You know I can't write a thing without my pen! And I can't tell your mother about it—she thinks that Lord Willy-Nilly is silly!"

"No problem," Eliza replied.

"Smashing!" Nigel exulted. "I took more boxes out of the other side of the Commvee. Be a love and dig through them!"

Eliza raced around the Commvee, the family's home on wheels. Darwin, who was used to trying to keep up with Eliza, followed.

Donnie, thinking they must be up to some new game, happily ran after them.

Upon reaching the other side of the Commvee, the three of them saw dozens of boxes on the ground. "What are we doing?" Darwin asked. Eliza quickly explained Nigel's dilemma to him.

Eliza was able to talk to animals, but it was a secret she kept from everyone. Darwin rolled his eyes. "I have to work through snacktime again?"

Eliza smiled as she poked through a box and put it aside. Darwin liked to complain, but Eliza knew he'd help her. As Eliza turned to the next box, Donnie gleefully took the first box and turned it upside down. He picked up a native Polynesian flute and tried to jab it into his hair. Eliza gently took it away from him. "Donnie, don't put things in your hair!"

"*Manadda lebazza?*" Donnie answered, puzzled, scratching his head again.

"I think you're just trying to help," she

said to Donnie as she cleaned up the mess he made, "but you're just making more work for us!" Donnie bobbed his head up and down, as though he were nodding. But then he took the second box and dumped that out as well.

"Well," Eliza sighed, "at least you dumped this one out before we looked through it."

Eliza and Darwin picked through the scattered items from the box. After a while, a Commvee window opened and Eliza's older sister peeked out. "Like, what are you doing?" Debbie asked, annoyed.

"Looking for Dad's Lord Willy-Nilly pen," Eliza explained. "Wanna help?"

"In this heat and sun?" Debbie responded. "*Teenage Wasteland* says that heat and sun ruins your skin! I've already got three and a half blotches! I'll help look, but in here!" The window closed again.

Eliza and her friends went back to their mission. But they all froze when they heard an animal noise from the nearest marsh, which they could just see through the trees and brush, perhaps fifty yards away. "Help!" it cried out.

Eliza jumped up. "Come on! An animal's in trouble!"

Darwin grabbed her arm. "Wait, Eliza! What about helping your father?"

Eliza looked at the boxes and bit her lip. What could she do? Finally, she turned and walked toward the brush. "I have to help if an animal's in trouble!" she declared. "I'm sure I can do it and still have time to help Dad!"

"I hope you're right," Darwin muttered, hurrying after her.

"*Mallagallagga!*" Donnie cried happily, racing to catch up as though it were a game of follow-the-leader.

Chapter 2

Eliza, Darwin, and Donnie stepped through the brush onto the muddy banks of the marsh. None of them saw any animals. "Oh, help!" came the voice again.

Looking down, Darwin saw a crocodile, who was little more than a baby. Darwin screeched and jumped behind Eliza. He knew a young crocodile's teeth were still sharp!

Eliza knelt down. "What's the matter,

little fella?" she asked the crocodile. "Where's your family?"

"They're gone!" he cried. "Hunters came and took them away! I hid and they didn't find me! But my burrow in the swamp mud fell in! And I'm not big enough to build a new one. Oh, if I don't get in the shade, the heat will cook me!" He looked up at Eliza. "Please help!"

Back in the Commvee, Debbie lifted up a couch cushion, didn't see her father's pen, and sat down in front of the mirror. In its reflection, she could see a touch of sunburn on her forehead. Behind her, Marianne ran footage of the Knysna lourie through the projector.

"Mom," Debbie asked, "my skin's totally dried up! What am I gonna do?"

Marianne, under pressure to finish the film, barely heard her. "Huh? Oh. Try the leaf of an aloe vera plant, honey. Or some swamp mud!"

"*Swamp mud?* Major gross!" Debbie exclaimed. "I need moisturizer, not fertilizer!"

Marianne sighed and ran the film through again. "Whatever you say, dear."

In the swamp, Darwin tugged at Eliza's sleeve. "Eliza, you don't have time to help this crocodile! You promised to help your father!"

Eliza looked at the croc, who looked back with big, sad eyes. "Darwin, we'll run back to the Commvee, grab a shovel, and dig a burrow real quick! We'll have plenty of time left!" She turned back to the croc. "Don't worry, we'll be back soon."

"Do you promise?" the reptile asked.

"I promise!" Eliza replied, turning for camp.

"*Crock-a-rocka-hoooeeeeah,*" Donnie said,

kneeling down to grab the crocodile's tail. Darwin grabbed Donnie at the last second and pulled him along after Eliza.

"You have to be careful, Donnie," Eliza heard Darwin say. "You're just the right size for crocodile lunch!"

Chapter 3

Eliza grabbed the shovel from where it rested against the side of the Commvee. Darwin and Donnie were right behind her as they headed toward the swamp once more. But before she could get out of camp, Nigel sprang in front of her, waving a handful of pens.

"I've tried all of these pens," he wailed. "None of them help me write!"

"It's okay, Dad," Eliza soothed. "We'll find it, I know we will!"

Nigel groaned and paced away.

"We're staying here to help, right?" Darwin asked. "Just like you promised?"

Eliza sighed. "Promises, promises! I just wish there was a way I could be in two places at once!"

She looked around, as though she might see an answer. When she saw Debbie sorting through a bag of makeup in the cool shade of the Commvee's awning, Eliza smiled. Darwin had seen that look before. "Oh, no," he said. "Don't tell me you have a plan!"

Eliza didn't answer. She walked over to Debbie. "Hey, Deb," she said, "I remembered hearing the *coolest* cure for blotchy skin!"

Debbie looked up. "Tell me!" she said. "We're going to Cape Town next, and I want all those big city hunks to see me at my most excellent! What's the cure?"

"Well, I read on some Web site," Eliza

began, "that nothing works as well as a mudpack made from real swamp mud! And I saw a perfect swamp for you right over there!" Eliza pointed to the swamp where she and her friends met the crocodile.

"Huh!" Debbie exclaimed, surprised. "Mom told me the same thing! But mud's just too icky for me. I won't go near it!"

Eliza leaned forward, squinting. "Hey, is that a new blotch on your nose?"

Debbie shrieked in terror, grabbed the shovel from her sister's hands and, still carrying the makeup bag, ran for the swamp! Eliza smiled, watching her go. Donnie scratched his head again as he stared at Debbie.

"I know what you're doing," Darwin said. "Debbie will go dig up mud, making a burrow for that crocodile without ever knowing it!"

"Pretty smart, huh?" Eliza said. "That

way I can stay here and help Dad!"

"But you forgot one thing," Darwin pointed out. "The second Debbie sees that crocodile, it's bye-bye burrow!"

Eliza thought about it for a second, then smiled again. "Well, that means someone will just have to follow Debbie and make sure that doesn't happen! Someone like you and Donnie!"

"Go back to that swamp and give that crocodile a chance to sink his teeth into me? Ohhhhhh, no," Darwin protested, waving his arms. "Crocodiles love chimp meat! Everyone knows that!"

"This is only a little crocodile, Darwin!" Eliza said, trying to convince him.

"What if his appetite isn't little?" Darwin asked.

Eliza gently punched him on the shoulder. "Come on, Dar," she said. "You're too tough to get eaten! You've met lions, tigers,

Komodo dragons, and snow leopards, and none of them have taken a bite out of you!"

Darwin puffed out his chest. "It's true," he said. "I am pretty tough."

"And this is the only way to save that crocodile!" Eliza pleaded. "Won't you help? For me? Your best, best, best friend?"

Darwin bravely saluted her. "Okay, I'll do it." His voice cracked a little as he added, "If Donnie and I can watch Debbie from far away."

"Yes!" Eliza pumped her fist into the air. "Thank you, Dar! Now you take Donnie . . ." But Donnie was already scampering into the brush toward the swamp, babbling joyfully.

Darwin panicked and raced after Donnie. "Donnie! Don't run off and leave me alone! Uh . . . you're not as tough as I am!"

Once her friends were gone, Eliza moved to one of the nearby boxes, and started again to help her father.

Chapter 4

Debbie stepped into the clearing around the swamp, and her sneakers sank quickly into thick, wet mud. "Eeeuugh!" she said, wrinkling her nose in disgust. "The things I do for beauty!" And she started to shovel mud into a bucket.

Darwin and Donnie hid in the trees behind her. Darwin couldn't see the crocodile, which was just fine with him. Donnie simply scratched his head.

Suddenly, something moved at the edge of the swamp. Its color matched the green of the weeds so well, it took Darwin a second to realize it was the crocodile. It had caught sight of Debbie and was curious about what she was doing.

Debbie was so focused on getting the mud that she didn't see the reptile inching closer to her leg! It was too far for Darwin to run and get there in time to distract her, so he did the thing he did best.

"*Eee! Eee! Eee!*" he screeched at the top of his lungs!

"*Zabbada whee! Zabbada zabbada whee! Zabbada whee!*" Donnie chimed in, having fun trying to copy his pal.

Back at the camp, Eliza heard the noises from the swamp and looked up. She knew something was wrong, and she was glad her parents were busy enough that they hadn't noticed the commotion. Eliza took a step toward the swamp. Just then, the Commvee door opened and Marianne poked her head out.

"Nigel!" she called. "The Foundation just radioed us! The courier plane is getting close!"

Nigel ran around the Commvee to look up at her. He hopped from one foot to the other, nervous. "That's splendid news, lovey!"

"Your script is almost done, right?" Marianne asked. "Telling the Foundation, 'The panther ate my film,' won't work this time!"

"Never fear, pumpkin," Nigel replied, faking a jaunty laugh. "I'll be finished in a trice!"

As Marianne closed the window, Nigel hurried over to Eliza. "Tell me you have good news, Eliza!"

Eliza looked toward the swamp, then back at her panicked Dad. "Nothing yet, Dad, but I promise we'll find it!"

Nigel's eyes grew misty. "Truly, a man couldn't wish for a better family! Always ready to help in a pinch! Come, let's investigate this box together!"

As Nigel threw himself into searching yet another crate, Eliza sighed. She knew there was no way to break away now. She simply had to hope Darwin and Donnie could take care of whatever was happening in the swamp.

Chapter 5

Debbie heard all the noises in the trees, and looked up from her digging. After a moment, she shook her head. "Probably just some samango monkeys fighting over a big banana," she muttered, and went back to digging.

In the trees, Darwin saw the crocodile inch closer to Debbie's leg. He knew he couldn't let Eliza's sister become a crocodile's feast! Eliza would never forgive him!

Darwin took a deep breath and reminded himself how tough he was. He didn't necessarily believe it, but someone in Eliza's family was in trouble, and he was the only one who could do anything about it. He grabbed a nearby vine and swung out over the mud.

Before he could reach Debbie, however, Donnie leapt out of the brush with a joyous whoop! Debbie turned just in time to see the boy cannonball into the deep mud, splashing it everywhere!

Darwin, swinging above the swamp, saw some mud cover the croc, which made him glad it was hidden; and he also saw a lot of mud splatter Debbie from neck to toe, which made Darwin smile.

But a second later he was splashed by the mud too. "*Eee-aah!*" he groaned, wrinkling his nose at the smelly mud.

"What the—Donnie!" Debbie spluttered.

"What are you—" Then she looked up and saw a mud-spattered chimp swinging overhead. "Darwin?"

Darwin smiled sheepishly.

Then the mud on the vine started to make his grip slippery, and Darwin could only whimper before he plunged into the swamp too, splashing everyone with mud—again! He came up spitting mud and saw Debbie glaring at him.

Darwin pulled Donnie out of the muck and hurried to the bank of the swamp, away from the crocodile. He tried to catch his breath, and decided he'd been tough enough for one day.

Debbie shook with frustration. "I'm covered in mud, and none of it is on my face," she said. "This is *not* the way to cure blotchy skin!"

Darwin simply stared at her, not understanding what she was saying.

Donnie scratched his head again.

Debbie looked down at the bucket. "That should be enough," she said. "If I need more, I can always peel it off my shirt!" She picked up the shovel and the bucket, and started back to camp.

Darwin and Donnie hauled themselves out of the swamp as the croc scrambled into the shallow trench Debbie dug. Darwin could see the trench wasn't nearly deep enough, and didn't protect the croc at all from the blazing sun. The little creature was in as much trouble as ever.

Chapter 6

Eliza and Nigel sat in the middle of camp, surrounded by trinkets and totems, shields and jewelry, and all of the other souvenirs from the Thornberrys' life on the road. They had gone through every box looking for the Lord Willy-Nilly pen, and it was still missing. Nigel knew there was only one thing to do.

"We have to start all over!"

Eliza sighed, but she knew he was right.

The pen had to be somewhere, they just hadn't seen it yet. "I'll start with these boxes again, Dad," she offered. "You look over there."

"We'll have to look twice as fast now," Nigel reminded her as he hurried away, "because we have half as much time!"

Eliza started searching, but a second later, Debbie walked back through camp, carrying her bucket of mud. Debbie saw her sister looking at her mud-caked clothes. "Don't ask," Debbie warned, before disappearing into the Commvee.

Eliza smiled. At least that was one thing she didn't have to worry about anymore. As long as she knew the crocodile was safe and sound, she could return to helping her father without any worry.

Just then Darwin and Donnie appeared, covered in mud like Debbie. Eliza smiled as they approached. "Everything worked out okay, just like I said it would, right?" she whispered to Darwin.

"Not even close," Darwin said. "Debbie didn't dig deep enough! You have to come and help!"

Eliza could see her father at the other end of camp, going through boxes. He looked helpless and desperate. "Eliza!" Darwin scolded her. "It's too late to think of another plan!"

But Eliza already had another plan. She ran inside the Commvee.

Inside, she saw Debbie digging her hands into the mud-filled bucket. Taking a deep breath, Debbie brought the mud to her face.

Eliza dove across the Commvee, knocking the goop out of Debbie's hands! Mud flew everywhere, even onto the shipping labels Marianne was filling out!

"Eliza!" Debbie and her mother shouted at the same time.

"Mom, I'm sorry," Eliza said hastily, "but Debbie, you can't put that mud on your face!"

"But you and Mom said—," Debbie began.

"Deb, that's surface mud," Eliza said, pointing to the bag. "Who knows what kinds of zit-causing germs are in there?"

"Whoa," Debbie said, looking at the mud. "That was close!"

"Good for you, Eliza, looking out for your sister like that," Marianne said, picking up her muddy mailing labels.

"You need mud from deeper down in the swamp," Eliza told her sister. "That's the stuff that's best!"

"No way!" Debbie said. "I'm not going back into that stinky swamp, or into that boiling sun for anything!"

"But Deb—"

Before Eliza could finish, Nigel burst in.

"Eliza! Any luck finding the pen?"

"Dad, I—"

And then she heard the buzz of a plane engine, getting closer to their camp. Eliza knew it was the courier plane coming for the film. And she also knew that keeping what seemed to be two simple promises looked like it was going to be impossible!

Chapter 7

Nigel's ears wiggled and his mustache twitched as he heard the plane as well. "Oh, no!" Then, catching Marianne's look, he said, "I mean, oh, splendid, the courier plane is almost here!" Nigel frantically ran out of the Commvee.

Eliza hurriedly turned back to her sister. "It's okay, Deb. I understand if you don't want to go back for more mud."

"Yeah, like you've ever understood me," Debbie snorted.

"No, I do," Eliza assured her. "Our next stop is Cape Town. You should probably just stay in the Commvee the whole time and not let those cute big-city boys see your blotchy skin. Why go out in the sun now for the only thing that might help you?"

Eliza watched Debbie wrestle with that thought for a moment. Then Debbie grabbed up the shovel and bucket, and stalked out the door. "All right," she grumbled. "But my skin better shine when this is all over!"

Eliza, Donnie, and Darwin followed Debbie out and watched her walk toward the swamp. Donnie scratched his head again.

"Okay, guys," Eliza said to her friends. "You gotta follow her one more time!"

"Eliza," Darwin begged, "please come along!"

"I can't, Dar!" she said. "Time is running out for Dad, and I made a promise to him first! But I can see everything that happens in the swamp from here, so don't worry!"

"Me? Not worry?" Darwin asked, pointing to himself. "Did you forget who you're talking to?" Then he took Donnie's hand and marched away.

Eliza dashed to the nearest box and dove into it, looking through knickknacks and notes. As she did, Marianne emerged from the Commvee carrying the tape recorder. "All right, Nigel," she called out. "We're ready to record your last few lines. And yes, you have to use your real voice this time!"

Nigel appeared from the other side of the Commvee, wringing his hands. "Oh,

smashing, smashing, really super of you to bring the recorder . . ."

Marianne squinted at him. "Nigel, why are you acting so funny?"

"Acting funny?" Nigel said, laughing loudly, clearly stalling for time. "Oh, Marianne, you're such a pip. Thinking I might be hiding something! Really!"

"Then let's record, so we can give this to the courier, all right?"

"Right, right," Nigel said, looking this way and that. "Just let me go around the Commvee and warm up my voice." He looked at Eliza in desperation, and dashed away. Eliza dove back into the box and dug even faster.

But something caught her eye as she dug, and looking up, she saw the swamp. There was Debbie, hard at work, digging beneath a tree. It looked like a branch was slithering above her head. Then

Eliza looked as hard as she could, and saw it wasn't a branch slithering—it was a snake! Soon she saw three of them, and Eliza knew they weren't just any snakes but *boomslangs*—poisonous vipers—slithering toward Debbie!

Chapter 8

Eliza leapt from the box and dashed out of camp toward the swamp. The snakes were swaying out of the tree, closer and closer to Debbie.

Approaching the swamp, Eliza hurried past Donnie and Darwin, and leapt into another tree, one with branches that intertwined with the tree Debbie stood under. Darwin and Donnie followed her up.

Eliza climbed high in her tree, fast enough to make Darwin proud, then jumped the short distance to the tree the snakes called home. Her friends followed.

They were above the snakes now, and Eliza scuttled down to a spot just over them. She reached down, but wasn't close enough to grab the snakes' tails.

She looked at Darwin, who nodded. He grabbed her ankles and lowered her down toward the snakes, very carefully.

It was hard work for Darwin to keep his place on the tree, but when he started to slip, Donnie grabbed him with one hand and held on to the tree with the other. He thought this was all part of a game they were playing. The three pals formed a living chain stretching down to the snakes.

The snakes' fangs were now inches from Debbie, who hadn't even looked up. Eliza reached as far as she could, then

bravely and quickly grabbed the snakes by their tails.

Just before they could turn and bite her, she flung the snakes as far away as she could. The boomslangs flew away, hissing angrily.

Eliza let out a huge sigh of relief, and looked down. Debbie was still clueless as she finished digging in her now-deep trench. Picking up the bucket full of mud, Debbie walked back to the camp.

Darwin hauled Eliza back up. "Thanks, guys," she told them, as they climbed down out of the tree.

They watched the crocodile move out of hiding and into the new burrow. It pulled back into the cool shade. "This is perfect," he said. "Thanks for your help!"

"I'm glad you like it," Eliza said, smiling.

"I'm gonna live here a long time," the crocodile said confidently.

Darwin tugged at Eliza's sleeve. Between the crocodile and the snakes, he had decided he'd been brave enough now for a whole week, maybe even a month! "Can we leave now?" he whispered.

Eliza put a hand on his shoulder, and another hand on Donnie's head. "We sure can! You guys did a great job today, and . . . ow!"

She pulled her hand back from Donnie's tangled hair. Something had poked her. "What is that?" she asked.

Donnie squirmed as Eliza poked through his hair. "*Yadda dabagga maggada ma!*" he protested.

"Hold still for a minute, Donnie," Eliza begged. "You've got all kinds of stuff in here!" She pulled out pebbles, sticks, a few bugs, and finally . . . a pen. And not just any pen . . .

"The Lord Willy-Nilly pen!" she cried,

holding it up. "That's where it's been the whole time! And now that I think about it, you *have* been scratching your head a lot lately, Donnie. I bet this is why!"

"*Oooh!*" Donnie said.

"We gotta get this back to Dad!" Eliza shouted. Then she raced away, her friends right behind her.

Chapter 9

Eliza leapt over nubby bushes and ducked under low branches as she sped back to camp. Darwin and Donnie scampered along beside her.

Donnie was having a terrific time—all this running back and forth between camp and the swamp had been a great game to him. "*Vrooma vrooma rumbadda vroom!*" he yelled.

Up ahead, Eliza could hear the angry

voice of the courier plane pilot. "Listen, I have a schedule to keep," she said, "and if your film isn't done, then you've missed your deadline, and that's all there is to it!"

"Please," Eliza heard Marianne say, "just wait a few more minutes! I'm sure Nigel will think of something we can record to end the film very, very soon!"

"Oh, yes," Nigel assured them in a none-too-sure voice. "I almost always think of something."

"Sorry, no," the pilot said. "I have to go now."

At that moment, Eliza burst out of the brush and ran smack into the pilot! "Oof!" they both exclaimed.

Eliza stumbled forward and the Lord Willy-Nilly pen was knocked out of her hand. As she landed on the ground, Eliza saw the pen tumble through the air . . . finally landing in the palm of Nigel's out-stretched hand!

Nigel looked at the pen in wonder, then smiled at Marianne, happy tears filling his eyes. "Now I know how King Arthur must have felt when he found Excalibur!"

Marianne pushed him to the picnic table. "Okay, *Arthur*, just pretend this is a Round Table and start writing!"

In the time it took Eliza and the pilot to stand up and brush themselves off, Nigel wrote furiously, then stood up. "Ready, Guinevere, I mean, Marianne!"

As the pilot checked her watch, Marianne moved her recorder into position. "All right, Nigel, you get one chance to get it right!"

Nigel nodded, Marianne turned on the tape recorder, and he began to speak, reading a few perfect lines to put the finishing touch on the film.

Marianne popped the tape out, put it inside the box with the film, closed the box, and handed it to the pilot. "See?" Marianne said to the pilot with a grin. "We finished in plenty of time."

The pilot harrumphed and walked off toward her plane.

Nigel hugged Eliza so tight she couldn't breathe. "Poppet!" he exclaimed. "Wherever did you find my pen?"

"Actually, Donnie found it," she replied, pointing at Donnie. "He really used his head."

"Excellent, Donnie," Nigel said, giving the boy a hug.

"*Beep, beep!*" Donnie said, squeezing Nigel's nose.

Marianne looked around at the messy camp, with boxes lying everywhere. "Now that we've turned in our movie, let's clean up this camp," she suggested.

"Splendid idea," Nigel agreed, following behind her.

Eliza plopped herself down heavily at the picnic table, and Darwin collapsed beside her. "Whew! I tell you, Darwin, next time I'll make sure I can keep a promise before I make one!"

"Or two," Darwin added. "I guess it's a good thing that crocodile is safe, even if it means a lot of other animals won't be when he gets bigger!"

Eliza smiled. "My dad got his pen, and that crocodile got his burrow. Everyone got what they wanted!"

At that moment, the Commvee door opened, and a hideous-looking monster jumped out! Its yellow hair flew in all directions, and its beady eyes peered out from under layers of dirt and mud!

Darwin yelped and leapt behind Eliza. But Eliza knew better than to be scared. After all, the monster was wearing her sister's clothes.

"Hey, Dweeberella," Debbie said from beneath her mudpack, "this mud stuff rocks! I can feel it working already! Wait till the boys in Cape Town get a load of my clear skin! They won't be able to resist me!"

"I'm sure you're right, Deb," Eliza agreed. "Just make sure you take off the mudpack before we get there!"

"Ha ha," Debbie said, rolling her eyes. "I'm going to put some more mud on, just in case." And she slammed the door as she went back into the Commvee.

Darwin peeked out from behind Eliza, who couldn't help laughing. "Yep, Darwin, everyone got just what they wanted!"

Discovery Facts

Hogsback: Hogsback is a town on South Africa's East Cape, located near the Amatola Mountains.

Knysna Lourie: Knysna louries are green birds with white crests that live in evergreen forests. They can be hard to see, but their "kow-kow-kow!" call is easy to hear!

Nile Crocodile: Adult Nile crocodiles can have between sixty-four and sixty-eight teeth! They are also called "Garwe" or "Ngwenya."

Boomslangs: Boomslangs are a species of South African snake that live in trees and feed on small animals. They can grow up to six feet in length!

About the Author

Adam Beechen has written scripts for episodes of the Nickelodeon animated shows *The Wild Thornberrys, Rugrats,* and *Rocket Power.* He is also the author of The Wild Thornberrys *Survival Guide* and lives in Los Angeles.

Adam has never met a real, live crocodile, but when he was three years old, he became close friends with a stuffed alligator that his neighbors had given him. It kept him company as it sat on top of the dresser in his room for many years!

1 GRAND PRIZE:

A 3-day/2-night trip for four to Nickelodeon Studios in Orlando, Florida

3 FIRST PRIZES:

A Sony Playstation® system and a *Rugrats™ in Paris* Playstation game from THQ®

25 SECOND PRIZES:

A *The Wild Thornberrys* CD-ROM from Mattel Interactive

100 THIRD PRIZES:

A set of four books from Simon & Schuster Children's Publishing, including a *The Wild Thornberrys* title, a *Rugrats* title, a *SpongeBob SquarePants* title, and a *Hey Arnold!* title

Complete entry form and send to:
Simon & Schuster Children's Publishing Division
Marketing Department/ "Nickelodeon Studios Florida Sweepstakes"
1230 Avenue of the Americas, 4th Floor, NY, NY 10020

Name_____ Birthdate___/___/_____

Address_____

City_____ State_____ Zip_____

Phone (____) _____

Parent/Guardian Signature _____

See back for official rules.

Simon & Schuster Children's Publishing Division/ "Nickelodeon Studios Florida Sweepstakes" Sponsor's Official Rules:

NO PURCHASE NECESSARY.

Enter by mailing this completed Official Entry Form (no copies allowed) or by mailing a 3 1/2" x 5" card with your complete name and address, parent and/or legal guardian's name, daytime telephone number, and birthdate to the Simon & Schuster Children's Publishing Division/ "Nickelodeon Studios Florida Sweepstakes," 1230 Avenue of the Americas, 4th Floor, NY, NY 10020. Entry forms are available in the back of *The Rugrats Files #3: The Quest for the Holey Pail* (12/2000), *Rugrats Chapter Book #10: Dil in a Pickle* (11/2000), *The Wild Thornberrys Chapter Book #2: Two Promises Too Many!* (9/2000), *The Wild Thornberrys Chapter Book #3: A Time to Share* (9/2000), *SpongeBob SquarePants Trivia Book* (9/2000), *SpongeBob SquarePants Joke Book* (9/2000), *Hey Arnold! Chapter Book #1: Arnold for President* (9/2000), and *Hey Arnold! Chapter Book #2: Return of the Sewer King* (9/2000), and on the web site SimonSaysKids.com. Sweepstakes begins 8/1/2000 and ends 2/28/2001. Entries must be postmarked by 2/28/01 and received by 3/15/01. Not responsible for lost, late, damaged, postage-due, stolen, illegible, mutilated, incomplete, or misdirected or not delivered entries or mail, or for typographical errors in the entry form or rules. Entries are void if they are in whole or in part illegible, incomplete, or damaged. Enter as often as you wish, but each entry must be mailed separately. Entries will not be returned. Winners will be selected at random from all eligible entries received in a drawing to be held on or about 3/30/01. Grand prize winner must be available to travel during the months of June and July 2001. If Grand Prize winner is unable to travel on the specified dates, prize will be forfeited and awarded to an alternate. Winners will be notified by mail within 30 days of selection. The grand prize winner will be notified by phone as well. Odds of winning depend on the number of eligible entries received.

Prizes: One Grand Prize: A 3-day/2-night trip for four to Nickelodeon Studios in Orlando, FL, including a VIP tour, admission for four to Universal Studios Florida, round-trip coach airfare from a major U.S. airport nearest the winner's residence, and standard hotel accommodations (2 rooms, double occupancy) of sponsor's choice. (Total approx. retail value: $2,700.00). Winner must be accompanied by a parent or legal guardian. Prize does not include transfers, gratuities, or any other expenses not specified or listed herein. 3 First Prizes: A Sony Playstation system and a *Rugrats* Playstation game from THQ. (Total approx. retail value: $150.00 each). 25 Second Prizes: A *The Wild Thornberrys* CD-ROM from Mattel Interactive. (Approx. retail value: $29.99 each). 100 Third Prizes: A set of four books from Simon & Schuster Children's Publishing, including a *The Wild Thornberrys* title, a *Rugrats* title, a *SpongeBob SquarePants* title, and a *Hey Arnold!* title. (Total approx. retail value: $12.00 per set).

The sweepstakes is open to legal residents of the continental U.S. (excluding Puerto Rico) and Canada (excluding Quebec) ages 5-13 as of 2/28/01. Proof of age is required to claim prize. Prizes will be awarded to winner's parent or legal guardian. Void wherever prohibited or restricted by law. All provincial, federal, state, and local laws apply. Simon & Schuster Inc. and MTV Networks and their respective officers, directors, shareholders, employees, suppliers, parent companies, subsidiaries, affiliates, agencies, sponsors, participating retailers, and persons connected with the use, marketing, or conducting of this sweepstakes are not eligible. Family members living in the same household as any of the individuals referred to in the preceding sentence are not eligible.

One prize per person or household. Prizes are not transferable, have no cash equivalent, and may not be substituted except by sponsors, in the event of prize unavailability, in which case a prize of equal or greater value will be awarded. All prizes will be awarded.

If a winner is a Canadian resident, then he/she must correctly answer a skill-based question administered by mail.

All expenses on receipt and use of prize including provincial, federal, state, and local taxes are the sole responsibility of the winner's parent or legal guardian. Winners' parents or legal guardians may be required to execute and return an Affidavit of Eligibility and Publicity Release and all other legal documents which the sweepstakes sponsors may require (including a W-9 tax form) within 15 days of attempted notification or an alternate winner will be selected. The grand prize winner, parent or legal guardian, and travel companions will be required to execute a liability release form prior to ticketing.

Winners' parents or legal guardians on behalf of the winners agree to allow use of winners' names, photographs, likenesses, and entries for any advertising, promotion, and publicity purposes without further compensation to or permission from the entrants, except where prohibited by law.

Winners and winners' parents or legal guardians agree that Simon & Schuster, Inc., Nickelodeon Studios, THQ, and MTV Networks and their respective officers, directors, shareholders, employees, suppliers, parent companies, subsidiaries, affiliates, agencies, sponsors, participating retailers, and persons connected with the use, marketing, or conducting of this sweepstakes shall have no responsibility or liability for injuries, losses, or damages of any kind in connection with the collection, acceptance, or use of the prizes awarded herein, or from participation in this promotion.

By participating in this sweepstakes, entrants agree to be bound by these rules and the decisions of the judges and sweepstakes sponsors, which are final in all matters relating to the sweepstakes. Failure to comply with the Official Rules may result in a disqualification of your entry and prohibition of any further participation in this sweepstakes.

The first names of the winners will be posted at SimonSaysKids.com or the first names of the winners may be obtained by sending a stamped, self-addressed envelope after 3/30/01 to Prize Winners, Simon & Schuster Children's Publishing Division "Nickelodeon Studios Sweepstakes," 1230 Avenue of the Americas, 4th Floor, NY, NY 10020.

Sponsor of sweepstakes is Simon & Schuster Inc.